Brick by Brick

A Snippet of the Life of Booker T. Washington

By: Louie T. McClain II
Edited by: Frank W. Minikon
Illustrated by: M. Ridho Mentarie

Also from Melanin Origins:

"Power in My Pen" – Ida B. Wells Fall 2016
"Genius Georgie" – George Washington Carver Spring 2017
"Free Your Mind" – Fredrick Douglass Fall 2017
"Louisiana Belle" – Madame C.J. Walker Spring 2018
Many more to come!!!

Hardcover Edition
ISBN: 978-1-62676-910-6

Publisher's Cataloging-in-Publication

(Provided by Quality Books, Inc.)

McClain, Louie T., II, author.
Brick by Brick : a snippet of the life of Booker T.
Washington / by Louie T. McClain II ; edited by Frank W.
Minikon ; illustrated by M. Ridho Mentarie.
pages cm
SUMMARY: Details the life and achievements of Booker
T. Washington.
Audience: Ages 9 months to
ISBN 978-1-62676-910-6

1. Washington, Booker T., 1856-1915--Juvenile
literature. 2. African Americans--Biography--Juvenile
literature. 3. Educators--United States--Biography--
Juvenile literature. 4. Tuskegee Institute--Juvenile
literature. 5. Biographies. [1. Washington, Booker T.,
1856-1915. 2. African Americans--Biography.
3. Teachers.] I. Mentarie, M. Ridho, illustrator.
II. Title.
E185.97.W4M328 2016   370.92
QBI16-600049

Dedication

Dedicated to my two little heart beats Serenity Vanessa and Uneoh Noah: your Daddy loves you. Everything that I do is for your health, wealth, and self-actualization. You are strong, beautiful, and unstoppable. The redemption in your eyes and fervor of your spirits gives me the strength and motivation to be the best man I can be.

— Louie T. McClain - Author

Dedicated to my beautiful and inspirational children Zair Rashad and Morgan Grace. You inspire me to progress and elevate my thinking, so that I might inspire and encourage you to make the world a better place. You are the breath that keeps me alive and the fire that burns in my heart.

— Frank W. Minikon - Editor

Brick by brick, we can get the job done by laying one brick at a time.

I believed in my friends.

And together we were able to do some great things.

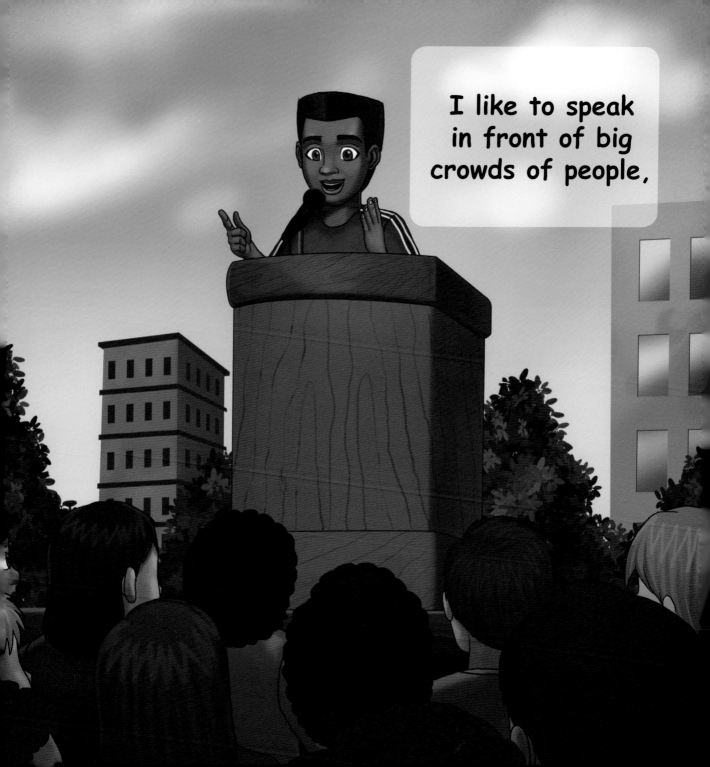

With the help of my friends, we built the Tuskegee Institute in Tuskegee, Alabama: a school for African American leadership.

People from all over the world seemed to like the special things that we were doing, so I helped them do the very same thing for their own families and friends.

Of course we can't forget
about playtime!

But you must always remember that you can do anything you set your heart to. You just have to take one step at a time, and build your dreams, brick by brick.

CASSEDY HALL, TUSKEGEE INSTITUTE. ERECTED BY STUDENTS.